To Z.D.H. Thanks for letting me feed
your soul with my cooking —W.B.

To my grandmothers, Lillian George and
Heriberta Ramos Esperanza —C.E.

The illustrations were made with oil on 16x20 Masonite board.

Cataloging-in-Publication Data has been applied for and
may be obtained from the Library of Congress.

ISBN 978-1-4197-4771-7

Printed and bound in China
10 9 8 7 6 5 4 3

Abrams Books for Young Readers are available at special discounts when purchased in quantity for premiums and
promotions as well as fundraising or educational use. Special editions can also be created to specification. For details,
contact specialsales@abramsbooks.com or the address below.

ABRAMS The Art of Books
195 Broadway, New York, NY 10007
abramsbooks.com

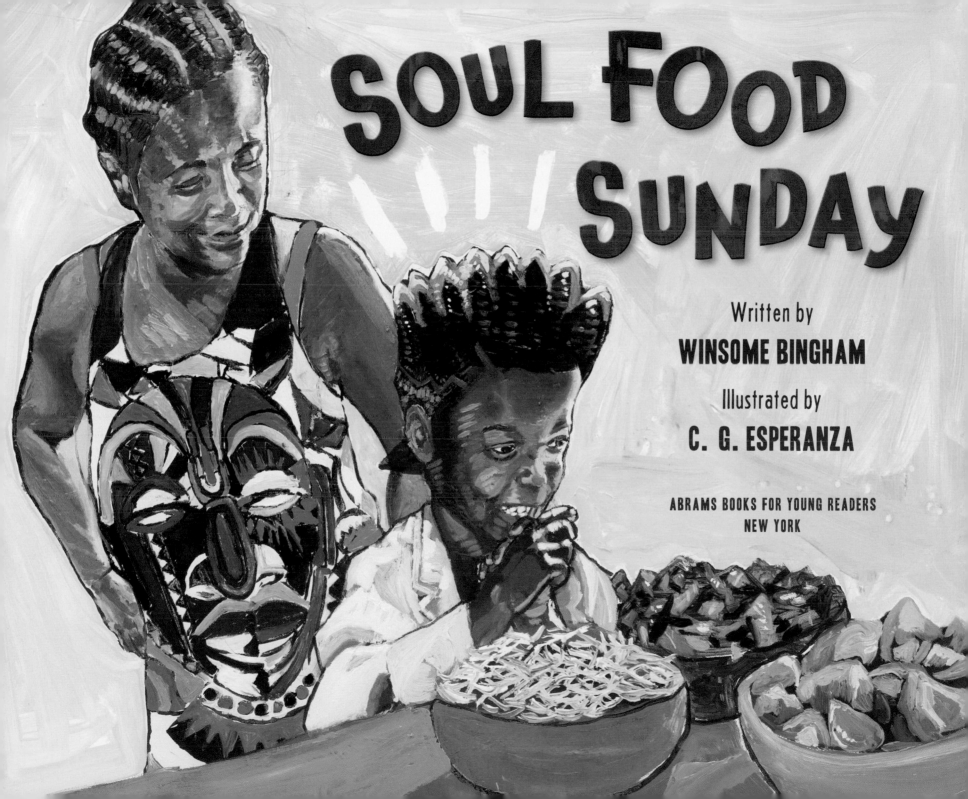

SOUL FOOD SUNDAY

Written by

WINSOME BINGHAM

Illustrated by

C. G. ESPERANZA

ABRAMS BOOKS FOR YOUNG READERS
NEW YORK

On Sundays, everyone gathers at Granny's for soul food.

The whole family is here.
Mommas and poppas,
aunts and uncles,
nieces, nephews, and a whole lot of cousins.

We park in the driveway and along the street.

Car horns   Car doors
BEEP!   SLAM!
Car alarms
CLOOK-CLOOK!

The men head to
the basement except
for Roscoe Ray.
He's the "Grill Master."

He has a spot
at the side of the
house. Everything he
needs is there. Grill. Coal.
Lighter fluid. CD player. Chair
with an umbrella. And a tiny
TV to watch football.

Granny goes in the kitchen with Momma and her sisters and straps on an apron.

The children sprint to the backyard or to the great room for video games.

But today, I don't go to the backyard or the great room.

I follow Granny instead.

"You're a big boy now," Granny says.
"Time for you to learn."
She hands me Grandpa's chef jacket,
the one he wore in the Army.
"Put this on, baby. And come with me."

Granny drops blocks of cheese on the table.

White cheese.
Yellow cheese.
Orange cheese.
Holey cheese.

"We need a whole lot of cheese. Unless mac 'n' cheese is on the table, it's not Soul Food Sunday."

Mmmmmm!

"I love mac 'n' cheese."

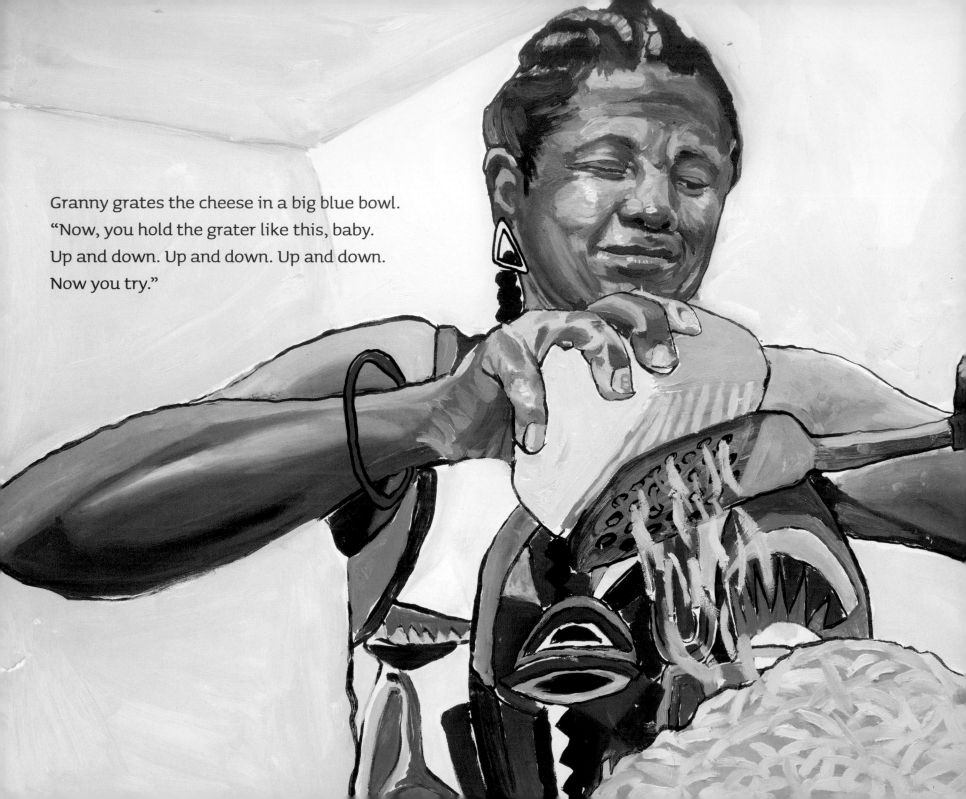

Granny grates the cheese in a big blue bowl.
"Now, you hold the grater like this, baby.
Up and down. Up and down. Up and down.
Now you try."

I grate. *Up and down.*
Up and down. Up and down.
"You got it, baby," says Granny.
"Now when you're finished,
come see me."

I grate and grate and grate.
My hand hurt.
My arm aches.
But I don't quit.

Cheeses stack high
like a mountain.
"I'm finished."

Granny checks my work. "Good job,
baby. That's the best grated cheese
I've seen in all my life."

"Greens is next." Granny pulls the greens from the bunch. "We need clean greens. A whole lot of greens, baby."

"Unless greens is on the table, it's not Soul Food Sunday."

Granny fills the sink with water
and vinegar and lemon juice.
"Greens got to be clean, baby,"
she says, scrubbing and shaking.

Collards.
Turnips.
Mustards.

Granny rubs the
leaves. They

squish
squish
squish

like she was hand-
washing clothes.
"I don't cook grainy
greens. This the only way
to get all the dirt out."

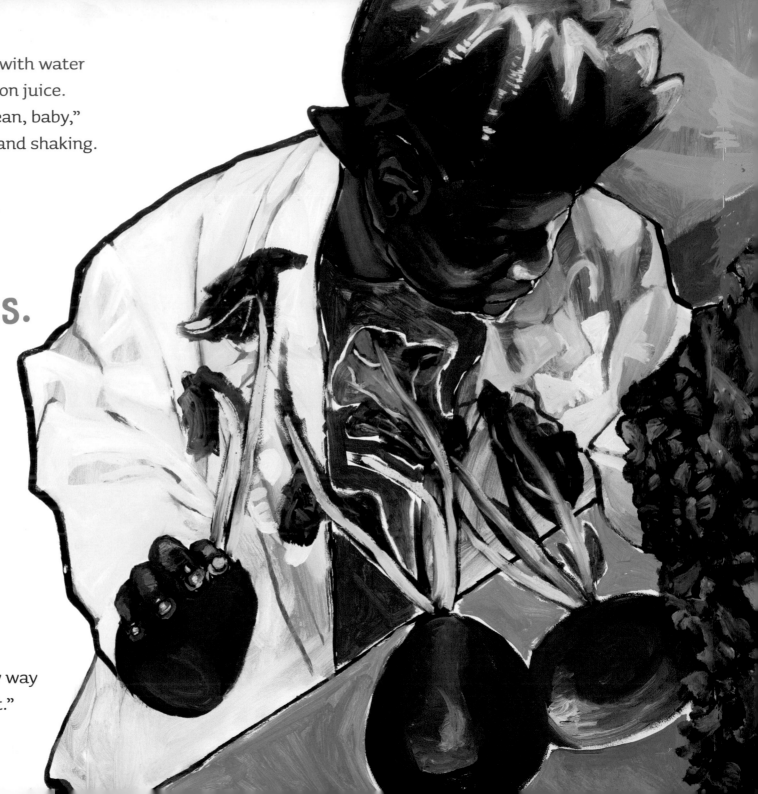

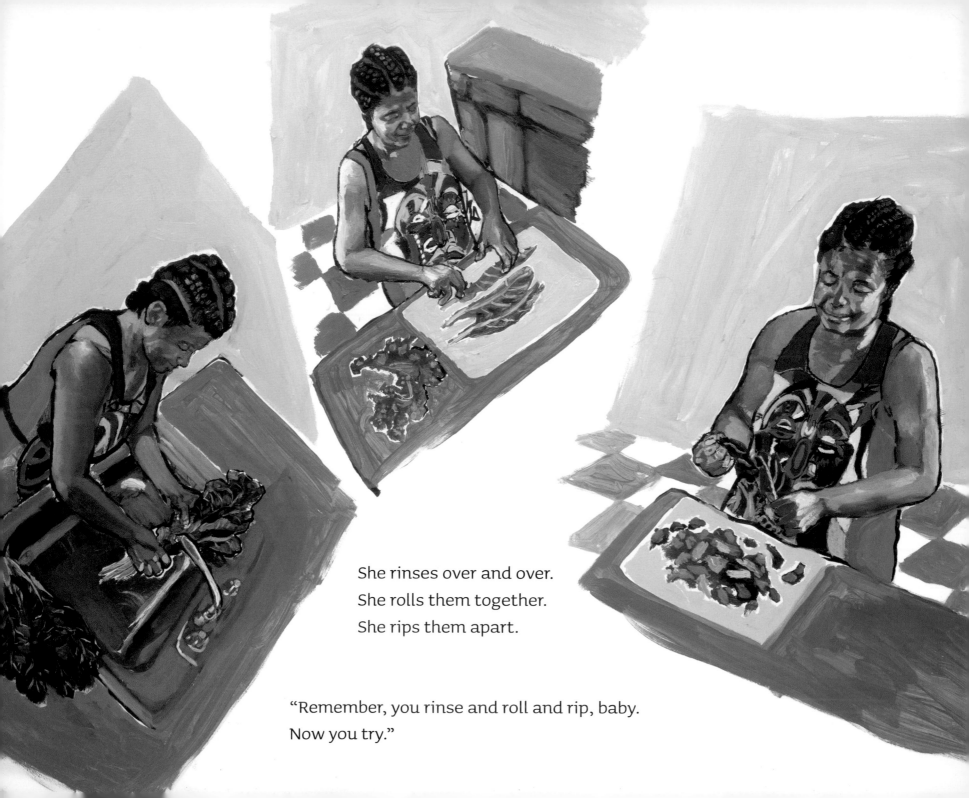

She rinses over and over.
She rolls them together.
She rips them apart.

"Remember, you rinse and roll and rip, baby.
Now you try."

I stand in front of the sink.
"I rinse and roll and rip."
"You got it, baby," says
Granny. "Now when you're
finished, come see me."

I rinse and rinse . . .

. . . and roll and roll . . .

. . . and rip and
rip and rip.

My hand hurt.
My arm aches.
But I don't quit.

Soon, greens pile high.

"I'm finished."

Granny checks my work. "Good job, baby.

That's the best greens I've seen in all my life."

"Roscoe Ray needs help with the meats," says Granny. "We cooking chicken and ribs and sausage. A whole lot of chicken and ribs, baby. Unless meat is on the table, it's not Soul Food Sunday."

Granny slaps sausage and slabs of ribs in the sink.

Pork ribs.
Beef ribs.
Hot and spicy
sausage links.

She skins the chicken.

She strips the membrane from the ribs.

She slices the sausage.

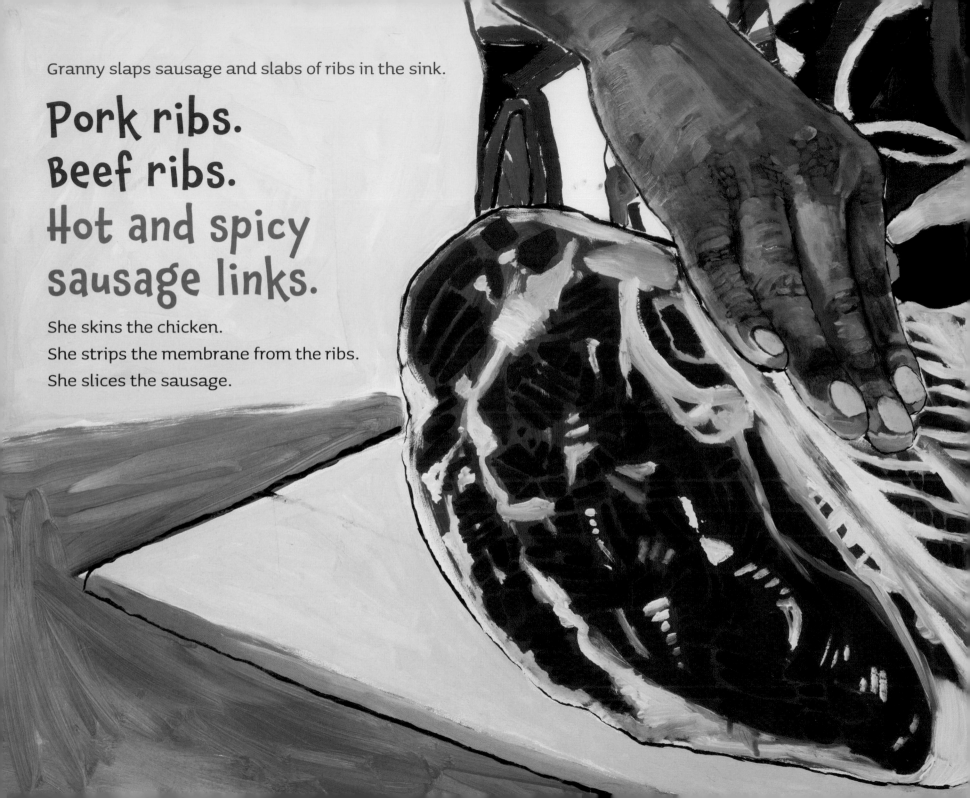

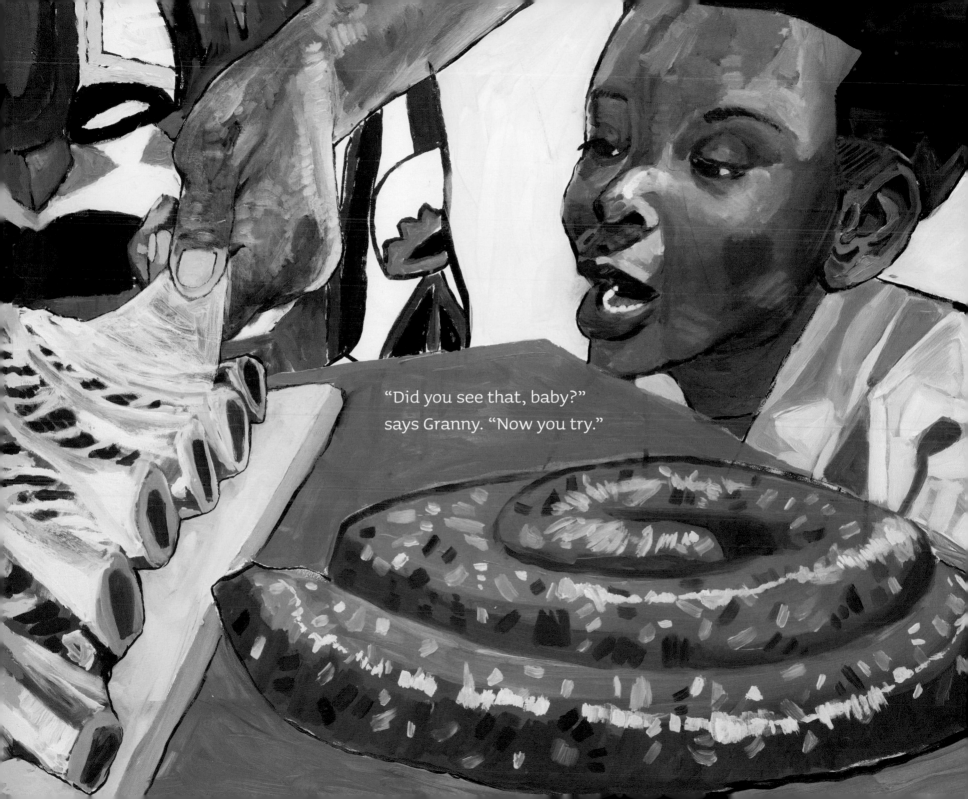

"Did you see that, baby?"
says Granny. "Now you try."

We switch places. "I skin the chicken.
I strip the membrane. I slice the sausage."
"You got it, baby," says Granny. "Now when
you're finished, come see me."

I skin and skin . . .

. . . and strip and strip . . .

. . . and slice and slice and slice.

My hand hurt.
My arm aches.
But I don't quit.

Soon chicken, ribs, and sausages
stack up next to the sink.
"I'm finished."

Granny checks my work. "Good
job, baby. That's the best-looking
meats I've seen in all my life."

"The grill is ready," Roscoe Ray yells.
He scoops the meat in a pan and
disappears through the side door.

"Well, everything is cooking now," Granny says. "We take a break. I take a nap. Your momma, God knows what she's about to do. But you, go on outside and play."

"But I don't want to play. I want to make something special."

Granny chuckles. "Baby, every food we make is special. Soul Food Sunday is about coming together. It's about us being family, working together, a team! And we have everything, baby."

"Well, everything is cooking now," Granny says. "We take a break. I take a nap. Your momma, God knows what she's about to do. But you, go on outside and play."

"But I don't want to play. I want to make something special."

Granny chuckles. "Baby, every food we make is special. Soul Food Sunday is about coming together. It's about us being family, working together, a team! And we have everything, baby."

Then I have an idea.

"I know something we forgot," I say.

"Do you need help, baby?"

"No, I can do it all by myself."

"Well, I will leave you be."

While Granny naps, I'm busy brewing . . .

Dropping ice.
Dunking tea bags.

Sugaring and
sweetening.

Lemoning
and liming.

And when I see Momma setting the food on the table, I put the jug next to the mac 'n' cheese and greens and ribs and chicken and sausages.

Granny comes down from her nap.
"I'm finished!" I tell her.

Granny sips. "Is this what I think it is?"

Then she takes another sip. And a gulp.

And two more gulps.

"This is the best tea I've tasted in all my life."

"Thank you, Granny," I say.

"Unless sweet tea is on the table, it's not

SOUL FOOD SUNDAY."

AUTHOR'S NOTE

I learned how to cook over the phone. It was the time before the Internet, so no YouTube or FaceTime; just a regular phone where you stuck your finger in the hole and moved the dial. My granny and aunties taught me how to cook. I would call Granny and ask her how to cook something. She broke everything down in steps. She would say, "Okay, baby. Listen. First thing you do is . . ." and then she'd say, "Call me back." I'd do just that and call her back. "Now, we do this . . . and call me back." Over and over, step by step, I followed and followed and followed all her instructions.

My granny walked you through the process. She had a style. She modeled. When we cooked together, she watched you imitate what she did. If you didn't do it the same way, she made you start over. And when you got it right, she filled your head with praise and positivity. Your cooking was a reflection of her. So, you better get it right. She always said, "When children know they do a good job, they will always do a better job the next time." There are many "Grannies" in the world teaching their children, grandchildren, and great-grandchildren how to carry on traditions and be self-sufficient.

One last thing: Never cook your greens before washing them in lemon juice and vinegar. The chemicals in the vinegar break down the dirt and drain its particles from the greens. No one should eat grainy greens.

ILLUSTRATOR'S NOTE

The aroma of a traditional soul food dinner teleports me back to my Grandma's house in the Forest projects in the Bronx on any Sunday in 1996. It helps me hear the sweet melody she would hum while she worked in the kitchen. The taste of soul food reminds me of how much she loved her family and how happy I am that she will always live on through the traditions she passed down. I hope this book will inspire magic moments between children and grandparents or the like for years to come. And also, more baked macaroni!

MAC 'N' CHEESE

INGREDIENTS

- 1 box (1 pound) elbow macaroni
- 1 block (8 ounces) sharp cheddar cheese
- 1 block (8 ounces) low-moisture mozzarella cheese
- 1 block (8 ounces) Monterey Jack cheese
- 1 block (8 ounces) Swiss cheese
- 2 tablespoons butter
- 2 tablespoons flour
- ½ teaspoon salt
- ¼ teaspoon pepper
- ½ teaspoon paprika
- ½ teaspoon Mrs. Dash (original)
- 1 cup heavy cream

STEPS

1. Ask an adult for help! Preheat the oven to 350°F (175°C).

2. Cook the macaroni in a pot of boiling salted water for 8 minutes, drain well, and set aside. Grate the cheeses, combine them in a bowl, and set aside.

3. Melt the butter in a saucepan over medium heat. Slowly add the flour, salt, pepper, paprika, and Mrs. Dash, stirring constantly. Then, while whisking, slowly pour in the heavy cream. A handful at a time, add ¾ of the grated cheese mixture, whisking constantly until the sauce is thick. Taste the cheese sauce with a spoon. Add more seasoning if needed. This is your creation. "ALWAYS TASTE YOUR FOOD WHILE COOKING. PEOPLE WILL REMEMBER YOU WERE THE COOK. LET IT BE A GOOD MEMORY, BECAUSE IF IT IS BAD, THEY WILL NOT LET YOU LIVE IT DOWN!" —GRANNY

4. Place the drained macaroni in a greased pan or dish. Fold in the cheese sauce and some of the leftover grated cheese. Add the rest of the grated cheese on top.

5. Put the macaroni in the preheated oven and bake for 35 minutes, or until the top is golden.